D0526460

WITHDRAWN
FROM
STOCK

*To Ann Bobco, with love*

SIMON & SCHUSTER
First published in Great Britain in 2017
by Simon & Schuster UK Ltd
1st Floor, 222 Gray's Inn Road, London, WC1X 8HB
A CBS Company

This edition published in 2018

Originally published in 2017 by Atheneum Books for Young Readers,
an imprint of Simon & Schuster Children's Publishing Division, New York

Text and interior illustrations copyright © 2017 by Ian Falconer
Jacket illustrations copyright © 2012, 2017 by Ian Falconer
Photo of Lincoln Center for the Performing Arts
copyright © 2006 by Magnus Feil
Photo of Park Avenue copyright © 2016 WallpaperFolder
All rights reserved

All rights reserved, including the right of reproduction
in whole or in part in any form
No reproduction without permission

The right of Ian Falconer to be identified as the author of this
work has been asserted by him in accordance with sections
77 and 78 of the Copyright, Designs and Patents Act, 1988

Book design by Ann Bobco
The text for this book is set in Centaur MT
The illustrations for this book are rendered in charcoal and gouache on paper

A CIP catalogue record for this book is available
from the British Library upon request

ISBN: 978 1 4711 6422 4 (hardback)
ISBN: 978 1 4711 6423 1 (paperback)
ISBN: 978 1 4711 6424 8 (eBook)

Printed in China

10 9 8 7 6 5 4 3 2 1

# OLIVIA
## the SPY

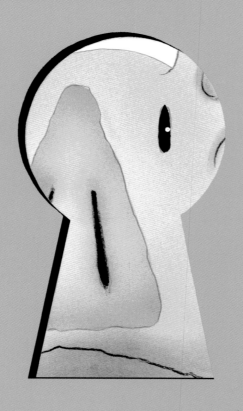

written and illustrated by Ian Falconer

**SIMON & SCHUSTER**
LONDON   NEW YORK   SYDNEY   TORONTO   NEW DELHI

Leabharlann
Contae na Midhe

One afternoon Olivia was
walking down the hall
when she heard her mother
talking to her aunt. "I'm
at the end of my tether.
I'd just finished cleaning the
kitchen when Olivia decided
to make a smoothie.
A *blueberry* smoothie."

Olivia, hearing her name,
paused to listen.

"I told her,
'Don't fill it up to the top.
Don't put all the blueberries in.
And not too much milk,
or then it will splatter!'"

"Mummy, I KNOW how to use the blender."

"Guess who had to clean *that* up?
Then," her mother continued,
"there was the episode with the laundry...

"I asked her to put her father's white shirts in the washer.

"'Olivia,' I said,
'put them in
one at a time
or else
they'll tangle . . .

"'. . . and only one capful of soap.'"

"Mother, I KNOW
how to work
the washing machine!"

"Olivia, you put your red socks
in with the white shirts,
and now the white shirts
are pink!"

"I think they
look pretty!"

"Well, then, *you* wear them!"

Which she did.

"Oh, I wish there was somewhere I could send her until she develops some SENSE!"

*Some SENSE?!* thought Olivia. *I'M the only one in this house with any sense! What ELSE is she saying about me? Maybe I should investigate.*

She decided to investigate.

But she had to be sneaky.

Olivia, who had always stood out, now needed to blend in.

She might be anywhere.

*Anywhere.*

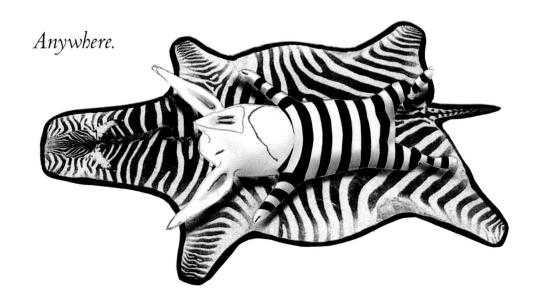

Seriously, anywhere.

Note: no mice, zebras, or lamps were harmed during the making of this book.

"Honestly, she's exhausting.
Yesterday I had to ask her five times
to clean up her room.

"If only there were someplace
where they could teach her to listen . . .

"like military school."

Olivia's mother had been planning to take Olivia to the ballet as a surprise, but now she was having second thoughts. "Do you think if I take her to the ballet, that she can sit through it without wiggling and squirming?"

Olivia sneaked around the corner just in time
to hear her father say, "Oh, that's the perfect place to take her!
After all, it's an INSTITUTION!"

The next day Olivia asked her teacher, "What's an institution?"

"That's a good question, Olivia.
An institution can be many things.
It can be a building, like a library,
or a tradition, like marriage.
Or it could be the military,
or a prison . . ."

library
marriage
the military
prison

# Prison?!

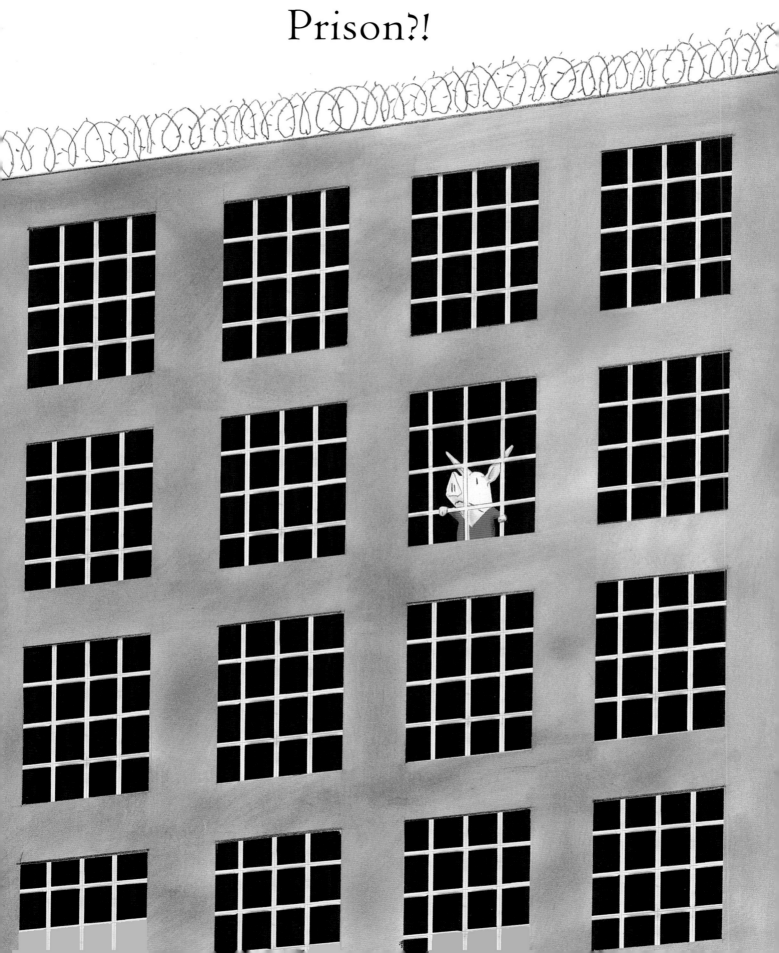

The next morning Olivia's mother told her
to be ready and dressed by six o'clock that evening.
"I'm going to take you somewhere SPECIAL!"

"Where are you taking me?" Olivia asked in a very small voice.

"It's a SURPRISE!"

"Okay, Mummy, I'll be ready."

All that sad day Olivia tried to figure out
what she would need for an institution.

She packed up her few pitiful possessions,
put on her best dress, and went downstairs.

"Oh, you can't take your *things*
where *you're* going . . .

"You're awfully quiet tonight, Olivia."

Olivia didn't answer.
She was saying goodbye to the city
she loved so well.

When they got out of the taxi, Olivia cried out,
"THE BALLET?! You're taking me to the BALLET?!"

"Yes, darling! That's the SURPRISE!"

"I thought you were taking me to an INSTITUTION!"

"*An institution?* Olivia . . . have you been eavesdropping?"

"What does 'eavesdropping' mean?" asked Olivia.

"It means listening to other people's conversations, sweetheart."

"Mummy, I would NEVER do that! I was SPYING!"

Before they took their seats, her mother asked her
if she needed to use the you-know-what.
"No," said Olivia, "I'm fine."

Of course ten minutes into the first act,
Olivia needed to use the you-know-what.

"Excuse me, my little one needs to use the you-know-what."

"Of course. It's the door on the left."

"Do you need me to come with you, Olivia?" her mother asked.

"I KNOW how to go to the bathroom, Mummy."

"I have one just that age. They can be a handful."

"They certainly can. You can't turn your back for one second."

"Not one single second!"

"There you are!" said Olivia's mother.
"You took such a long time, I was getting worried."

"It was a lot further away than the lady said."

"Thank you, Mummy. That was beautiful."

"Darling, I'm so glad you liked it."

"Although," Olivia added, "the girls in the *pas de quatre* could have worked on their *entrechats*."

"I'm sorry, Mummy.
I'll cook dinner all next week."

"Oh no you won't!"
said her mother.

"MUMMY,
I KNOW how to COOK!"

The End

(at least until tomorrow)